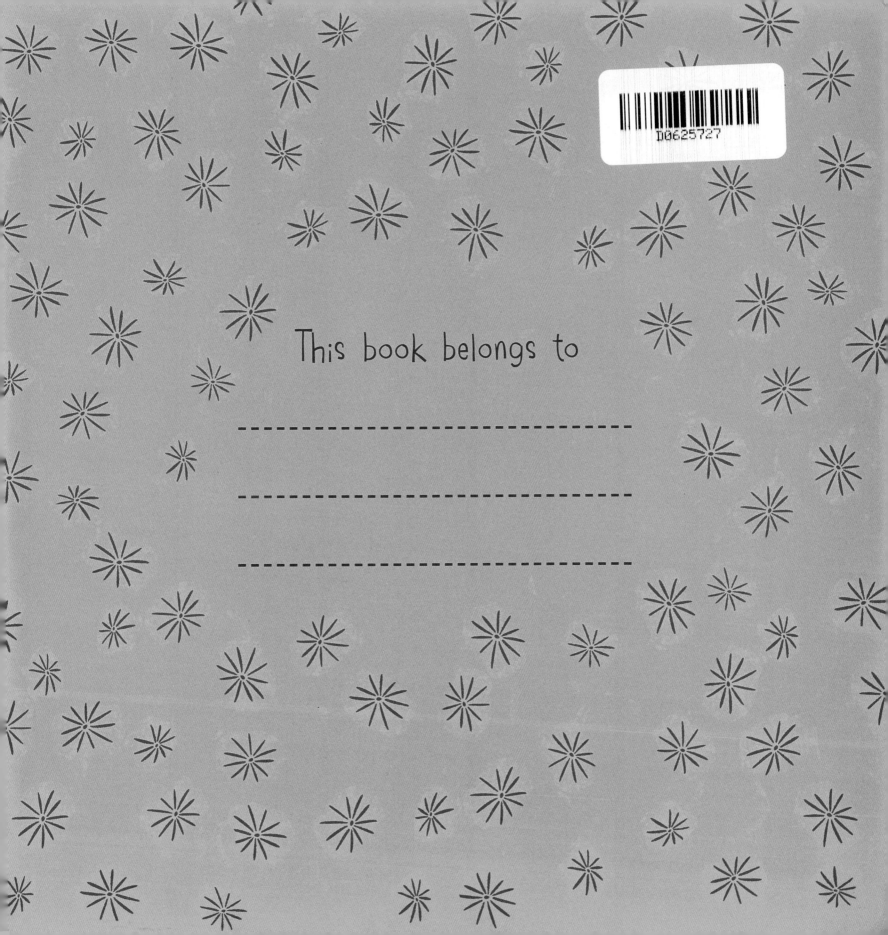

This book belongs to

Princess Shiloh   Princess Adanna   Princess Thandie   Princess Shaya   Princess Shanique

Princess Sade   Princess Kenya   Prince Rakim   Prince Dante   Prince Shaheed

For Ethelda 'Ms Ettie' McKenzie and
my singing sister Natalee.

H. L.

For my parents for encouraging
me to do what I love.

A. F.

FABER has published children's books since 1929. T. S. Eliot's *Old Possum's Book of Practical Cats* and Ted Hughes' *The Iron Man* were amongst the first. Our catalogue at the time said that 'it is by reading such books that children learn the difference between the shoddy and the genuine'. We still believe in the power of reading to transform children's lives. All our books are chosen with the express intention of growing a love of reading, a thirst for knowledge and to cultivate empathy. We pride ourselves on responsible editing. Last but not least, we believe in kind and inclusive books in which all children feel represented and important.

First published in the UK in 2021
First published in the US in 2021
by Faber and Faber Limited, Bloomsbury House,
74–77 Great Russell Street, London WC1B 3DA
Text © Hannah Lee, 2021 Illustrations © Allen Fatimaharan, 2021
Designed by Faber
US HB ISBN 978–0–571–36114–4
PB ISBN 978–0–571–36115–1
All rights reserved.
Printed in India
10 9 8 7 6 5 4 3 2 1
The moral rights of Hannah Lee and Allen Fatimaharan
have been asserted.
A CIP record for this book is available from the British Library.

The Rapping Princess

Hannah Lee Allen Fatimaharan

faber

Here is a story that everyone should know.
It's the tale of a princess named Shiloh.
She lived in a kingdom, not far from yours,
in a grand house with a swimming pool and fourteen floors.

I know that sounds too big but here's the thing:
her mother and father were the Queen and King.

Being a princess is a tough job for someone so small.
It's even harder when you have a problem you can't solve at all.

You see, every princess in the kingdom could sing.
Yet Shiloh's voice could do no such thing.

She went to the palace doctor who checked her voice box.
The doctor shrugged and said, "I see no major blocks."

The best vocal coach was called for, his instruments he brought.
"Sorry Shiloh," the teacher sang, "Talent can't be taught!"

One day, as Shiloh was coming back from class,
she heard sounds that she felt she couldn't pass.

Visiting princes made beats on their hands and chest,
they were battling to see who could rap best.

"It's me! It's me!" yelled Prince Rakim.
"Who can rap best? I am him!"

"You can't rap,
I'm cold like ice,
everyone agrees,
Prince Dante is nice."

"Your flow? Ha! Well I'm hot like the sun,
I'm Prince Shaheed, and I'm number one!"

Their rhymes sounded good enough,
but Shiloh could think of better stuff.
Suddenly Shiloh wasn't so shy.
She wanted to rap, she wanted to try!

"You've all got talent, yes that's agreed,
but can you match super Shiloh's speed?
See the way that I flow, that I dip, flip and rhyme?
I think you'll find Shiloh is most sublime."

The Princes clapped at what they saw.
"Shiloh can rap!" They were in awe.

Still Shiloh was sad: she couldn't sing!
That was what she wanted more than anything.

She tried smelly juices and ancient remedies,
but these just made her cough and sneeze.
Shiloh worked on her singing, day and night,
yet she just couldn't seem to get it right.

Shiloh wondered aloud, "Could it be?
My sisters got all the talent and left none for me?
The most beautiful sounds come from each throat,
but when I try to sing, I sound like a goat!"

"Your voice chose you," chimed the wise Queen and King.
"Perhaps you are just not meant to sing."

Shiloh cried, "Why am I the only one?
I can't sing and that's no fun!"

"Adanna belts songs
and I want to sing along.

Thandie's tender notes
never sound wrong!"

"Shaya scats and hums to every beat,

Shanique's voice is a soulful treat!"

"Sade's sweet soprano,

Kenya's cool contralto,
voices I wish I had, too.

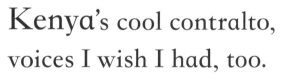

Why can I not sing? What should I do?"
"Stop this child, do not look and compare,
search yourself, your talent is there!"

Shiloh ran into her bedroom to cry.
She looked in the mirror and asked it, "Why?"

To her surprise, the mirror
spoke back and said . . .
"I think that you should stick
to rapping instead."

"So you cannot sing, that may be true,
but there are other things that your voice can do.

No need for tests, everything's fine.
Your voice is unique, your rapping's divine!

Your own talent scares you, you didn't realise before,
but each time you practise, you want to rap more."

Shiloh hadn't thought about it from that
  point of view.
Rapping was exactly what she wanted to do!
She loved to freestyle over a handmade beat,
unleashing lyrics to the tapping of her feet.

"I love to rap, it's when I have the most fun,
I've had talent all along though I thought I had none!"
Shiloh sent a message, she spread the word around.
"Come and listen to the voice that I have found!"

The palace was packed with guests from near and far.
They came in carriages, canoes, balloons, by car . . .

Everyone cheered as Shiloh took the stand.
Her sisters sang back-up, they were her band!
Shiloh switched skilfully between flows.
She amazed everyone with the words that she chose.

Her words jumped up and leapt,
they danced in the air,
she performed with such courage,
such confidence, such flair.

Everyone rose to their feet, they cheered with pride,
for Shiloh had found a voice she would not hide.

"It's mine, it's mine!" Shiloh yelled in delight.
"My voice has power! My voice has might!

My voice is strong, my voice is true,
I'm proud of the things my voice can do!"